A GOLDEN BOOK • NEW YORK

Baby Dear copyright © 1962 by Random House LLC
We Help Mommy copyright © 1959 by Random House LLC
Mommies: All About the Work They Do text copyright © 1997 by Margo Lundell
Illustrations copyright © 1997 Paul Meisel

All rights reserved. This 2015 edition was published in the United States by Golden Books, an imprint of Random House Children's Books, a division of Random House LLC, 1745 Broadway, New York, NY 10019, and in Canada by Random House of Canada Limited, Toronto, Penguin Random House Companies. The works that appear herein were originally published separately in 1959, 1962, and 1997. Golden Books, A Golden Book, A Little Golden Book, the G colophon, and the distinctive gold spine are registered trademarks of Random House LLC.

randomhouse.com/kids
Educators and librarians, for a variety of teaching tools, visit us at RHTeachersLibrarians.com
Library of Congress Control Number: 2014930718
ISBN 978-0-385-39273-0
MANUFACTURED IN CHINA
10 9 8 7 6 5 4 3 2

Baby Dear

By ESTHER WILKIN

Illustrated by
ELOISE WILKIN

Baby Dear is my brand-new baby doll.
Daddy brought her to me on a very special day.

It was the day he brought Mommy and our new baby home from the hospital.

Mommy loves her baby.
And I love mine.

We give our babies their bottles.

Then we pat their
backs to bubble them.

Mommy changes her baby.

And I change mine.

Mommy bathes her baby.
And I bathe Baby Dear.

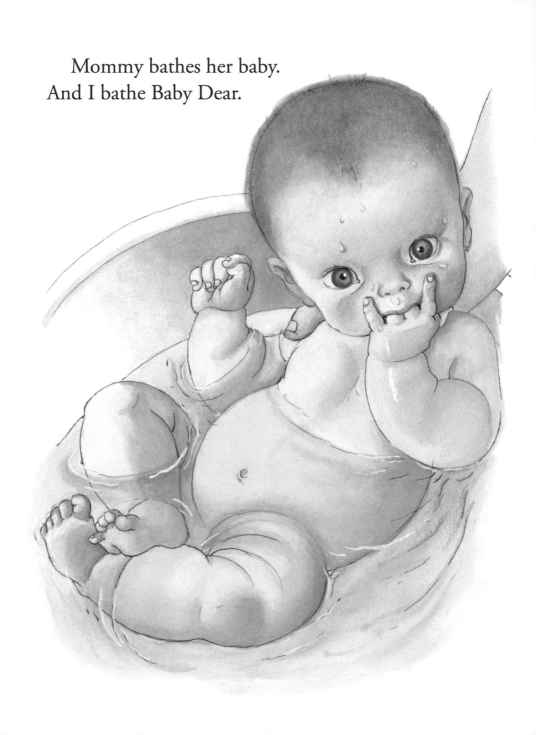

We play Little Piggy
with their little pink toes.

We dress our babies in their bonnets before we take them out.

Mommy has a carriage for her baby. And I have one for Baby Dear.

We go walking together with our babies.

Mommy's baby sleeps in the little white bed that used to be mine.

My baby sleeps in a cradle all her own.

Mommy has a book for
her baby and I have one
for Baby Dear.

We write things in our books about our babies.

Mommy sings to her baby and I sing to mine.

We smile at our babies and talk to them.
Mommy says this is the way our babies know
they are the most wonderful babies in the world.

Sometimes Mommy lets me hold her baby. Mommy's baby is my baby sister.

When my baby sister is a big girl
I will let her hold Baby Dear.

We Help Mommy

By JEAN USHMAN • Illustrated by ELOISE WILKIN

We help Mommy every day.
We help her in the morning, as soon as we get up.
We take off our pajamas.

Bobby puts on his pants, and socks, and shoes.
He can dress himself. I put on mine.
Over my head goes my shirt.
Oops! My arm is stuck.
Mommy will help me pull it out.

Mommy ties my shoes.
"You're a good girl, Martha," says Mommy.
"You can almost dress yourself."

We all go down for breakfast.
Bobby breaks the eggs for Daddy to fry.
I put bread in the toaster.
Out it pops, hot and brown!
"You two are a big help," says Daddy.

We wave good-by to Daddy from the door.
Then it's time to make Mommy's bed.
"Pull the sheet tight," Mommy says.
We pull until there's not a wrinkle left.
"Thank you," says Mommy when we're done.

Swish! swish! goes the broom.
Pfuff! pfuff! goes the dust mop.
Brr! brr! goes the carpet sweeper
as it picks up the dirt.

We are cleaning house.
Under the beds, over the rugs,
in all the corners we clean.
"Here is a dustcloth for you," says Mommy.
Bobby dusts the table-tops
while I mop under the chairs.

Now it's time to wash.
We collect the clothes.
Bobby puts Daddy's clothes
in the washing machine.
I put my dolly's clothes in.

In goes the soap.
Bang! goes the door.
Hmmmmm! goes the machine.
Round and round the clothes go.
I can see my face in the shiny glass.

My clothesline isn't high like Mommy's.
It is just right for me.
I hang up dolly's clothes.
Two clothespins for her dress.
One clothespin for each sock.
And one clothespin for her hat.

We see Ann and Jerry playing
in their sandbox next door.
"Come on over, Martha and Bobby!" they call.
"Run along," says Mommy.
"Take your pails and shovels.
Have fun!"

Once a week we go to the supermarket.
I ride in the cart while Bobby pushes.
Up and down the aisles we go.
"What would you like today?" asks Mommy.

We tell her cereal and apples
and cookies and raisins and a picture book.
We pile them on the counter.
Mommy has two big bags
and Bobby and I have little bags to carry home.

We like to put things away for Mommy.
The cereal goes in the cabinet,
the apples in the basket,
the cookies and raisins on the shelf.
"You're a big help," says Mommy.

Soon it is time for lunch.
Mommy gets the bread and cheese and meat.
I spread butter on two slices.
Bobby puts meat and cheese on two others.
Slap! Mommy puts them together.
What yummy sandwiches!

Now we set the table.

A place mat for Mommy.
And place mats for Bobby and me.
A knife and fork for Mommy.
A fork for each of us.
Napkins for us all.

After lunch Mommy washes the dishes.
She lets me dry the forks and spoons.
"Here's a spoon for you, Martha."
I take it from the dish rack
and rub it all over gently.
Bobby puts the dishes away.

I sit on a stool when I help Mommy bake pies.
Mommy mixes the dough in a big bowl.
She gives me a little ball of dough
to make a treat for Daddy.

Roll, pat. Roll, pat.
I'm making a treat for Daddy.
It's a funny man, with two cherries for eyes,
and one cherry for a mouth.
"Daddy will be very pleased," says Mommy.
And she puts it in the oven.

We've had a busy day helping Mommy.
Soon it is time to put away our toys
and books and clothes and get ready for bed.

We sing our put-away song:
In the box we put the blocks,
The dolls go in the crib;
Teddy Bear sits on the chair—
Puts on his bright blue bib.

Daddy comes to say good-night and tuck me in.
"That was a delicious treat, Martha," he says.
"Thank you both for being such a big help
to Mommy and me.
Sleep tight."

MOMMIES
All About
the Work They Do

By MARGO LUNDELL

Illustrated by PAUL MEISEL

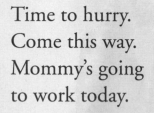

Time to hurry.
Come this way.
Mommy's going
to work today.

CAUTION
PEOPLE
WORKING

PHONE COMPANY

What kind of work
do mommies do?
Every sort of job.
It's true.

Many mommies
spend their hours
inside giant
office towers.

Some run a train.

And some stand up
in church and preach.

Some mommies really like to teach.

Others want
to work outside
in places where
the sky is wide.

Some drive a truck.

Some haul a tow
when cars get stuck.

Musician mommies
love to play.

Sculptor mommies
model clay.

Mommies farm
like daddies do.

They raise corn
and cattle, too.

Mommies are buyers.

Others are sellers.

Some handle money
and work as bank tellers.

Moms deliver.

Moms design.

Moms decide
who pays a fine.

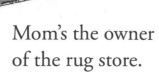

Mom's the owner
of the rug store.

She's the druggist
in the drugstore.

Doctor, dentist,
tennis player,
soldier, sailor,
city mayor.

Busy mommies!
What a list!
Now think of jobs
that we have missed.

But when the workday ends,
what then?
The mommies come
back home again.

Your mommy comes.
Her work is done.
You see her
and begin to run.

When she was gone,
what did you miss?
You simply wanted . . .

Mommy's kiss.